To Rachel Marie Anselmo, my beautiful sister. You were taken from us far too soon, Sister Bear. I love your adorable Henry and precious Sophia to the moon and back.

www.mascotbooks.com

Queen Celine's Vaccine Machine

©2019 Dr. Kevin R. Gendreau. All Rights Reserved. No part of this
publication may be reproduced, stored in a retrieval system or transmitted
in any form by any means electronic, mechanical, or photocopying,
recording or otherwise without the permission of the author.

For more information, please contact:
Mascot Books
620 Herndon Parkway #320
Herndon, VA 20170
info@mascotbooks.com

Library of Congress Control Number: 2018909838

CPSIA Code: PRT1118A
ISBN-13: 978-1-64307-055-1

Printed in the United States

Queen Celine's Vaccine Machine

Dr. Kevin R. Gendreau

illustrated by Juan Diaz

Far, far away in a queendom named Aires,
a land full of berries, canaries, and fairies,

A beautiful nurse whose name was Celine,
lived a beautiful life as the Queen of Vaccines.

Celine ensured children throughout her great land
got all their vaccines just as she had planned.

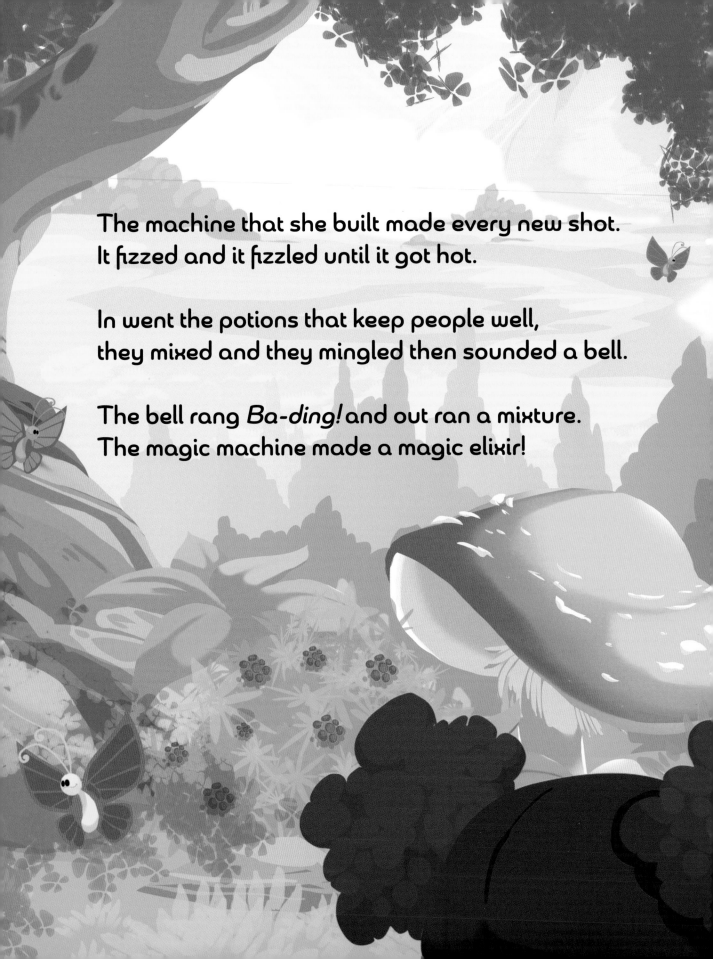

The machine that she built made every new shot.
It fizzed and it fizzled until it got hot.

In went the potions that keep people well,
they mixed and they mingled then sounded a bell.

The bell rang *Ba-ding!* and out ran a mixture.
The magic machine made a magic elixir!

Into small tubes for nurses to squeeze
went all of these liquids that help stop disease.

Her magic elixir comes in a small shot.
In your arm or your bum, it makes barely a dot.

Goodbye scary things, like measles and mumps,
that are known to hurt children with fevers and bumps.

So long chicken pox, and your silly red rash.
So long to those spots that make children scratch.

We hate all the coughing, we hate feeling groggy.
So scram now, pertussis, you bark like a doggy.

Ta-ta to you, tetanus, you make muscles tight.
You're a naughty disease that few kids can fight.

Farewell to the chills and the aches of the flu.
Farewell coughs and fevers, we bid you *adieu*.

With every new year and with every vaccine
the magic machine would need to be cleaned.

Celine started dusting, and then saw a spark,
and all of a sudden, its lights became dark!

"Oh no!" cried Celine, "I think it just broke!"
"It's creaking and squeaking. There's even some smoke!"

The whole village gathered when they heard her cry.
"Now what will we do? How will we get by?"

They knew the elixir prevented disease.
They could not remember the sound of a sneeze!

The sniffles and rashes had been kept at bay.
Vaccines kept them healthy to laugh, run, and play!

The villagers quietly looked at Celine,
who speedily shared an impeccable scheme:

"A cute little family, the cutest of all,
with two perfect children, so cute and so small.

Adorable Henry and precious Sophia,
so smart and so sweet with their puppy named Mia.

Those two little ones, they'll help save the day,
so kids don't get sick and can laugh, run, and play.

Find me those children and
        bring them here quickly.
I'm scared these diseases will
        make us all sickly!"

The two little cuties stepped out from the crowd,
and ran up to the queen, where both of them bowed.

"Sophia and Henry, you take things apart.
You put things together and help them to start!

Here are some tools, our machine needs some fixing.
As you have heard, our vaccines are not mixing!"

They banged on the bottom and tapped on the top.
They turned on the crank like stirring a pot.

The small hands of Henry both bolted and screwed,
and precious Sophia then started the fuse.

The machine began working to make a new shot.
It fizzed and it fizzled until it got hot!

The bell rang *Ba-ding!* and out ran a mixture.
The magic machine made a magic elixir!

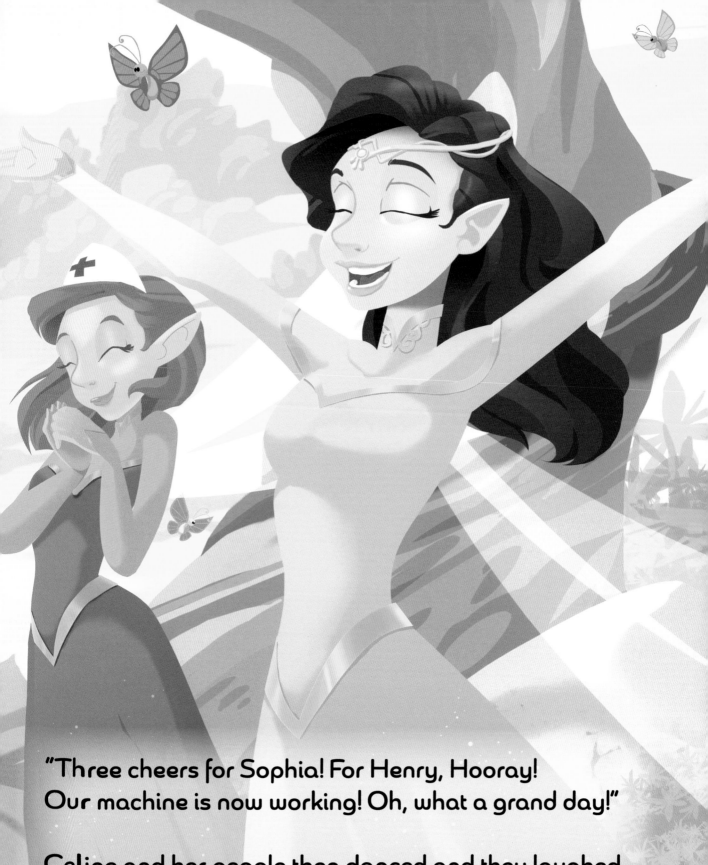

"Three cheers for Sophia! For Henry, Hooray!
Our machine is now working! Oh, what a grand day!"

Celine and her people then danced and they laughed.
They jumped really high and they ran really fast.

Far, far away in a queendom named Aires,
a land full of berries, canaries, and fairies,

Lived two little children, so precious and smart,
with a magic machine that they helped to restart.

The villagers felt safe to travel and play,
they joked and they laughed and they skipped
every day!

Acknowledgments

Sophia and Henry—thank you for being the source of our strength. You are our sunshine on the cloudiest of days.

Mom—thank you for being the rock of our family and the most caring person in the world.

Monique Borges—thank you for serving as inspiration for my new favorite fictional character.

Jacob Anselmo, Ashley de Padua, and Evan Glasson—thank you for your input, edits, and endless support!

About the Author

Kevin R. Gendreau , MD is a primary care physician and children's book author from Fall River, Massachusetts. Dr. Gendreau enjoys creative writing, preventative medicine, and long walks on the beach with his puppy, Teddy. He spends as much free time as possible with his niece and nephew, Sophia and Henry. He is passionate about discussing healthy diet and exercise plans with his patients, as he himself has lost 125 pounds with lifestyle modifications alone. Dr. Gendreau's first children's book, *A Healthier You with Sophia & Sue*, was also published by Mascot Books in 2012.